Jo and Alex Meet for the First Time

By L.S. Winters

Cover Illustrations by Mary Tsoukali

DEDICATION

This book is dedicated to my Mom and Dad. Thank you for everything.

ACKNOWLEDGMENTS

Thank you to all the family and friends who've supported and encouraged me during this process. I love you.

CHAPTER ONE

Jo is bored. Jo is almost always bored. The people on her street are boring. The kids at school are boring. She wants something interesting to happen. She sits on her porch swing and stares at the houses lining the street. Maybe something interesting will happen today.

Her cat, Jimothy, joins her on the swing and curls up next to her.

"Good morning, Jim. How're you today?"

Jim meows, and Jo nods.

"I agree. The weather is out of season. Hopefully, it'll be warm all day. I don't want to wear the itchy cardigan Gramma made me."

Jim meows again and jumps down. Jo sighs and watches as he strolls away. Even Jim is boring today. Luckily, she planned ahead. She brought a book and her drawing pad. She likes reading; she's good at it. She likes drawing, but she's not good at it. She doesn't mind. She doesn't show her drawings to anyone.

She opens the book and starts to read. The book is good, and it makes her laugh a lot. The sun is warm. Her mouth feels dry, so she goes inside for a glass of lemonade. When she gets back to the porch, there's a new car in front of the empty house two doors down.

She watches with interest as a large truck pulls up, and a family climbs out of the car. There are four people: A Mom, a Dad, and two girls. One of them is older, and she has a pair of headphones on. She's pretty, Jo thinks. Tall, big curly hair, wearing cool clothes. The other girl looks like she's Jo's age. From the distance, she looks as though she is Jo's height and has a big curly ponytail.

Finally, Jo thinks with relief. *Something interesting is happening! Maybe one of them will be less boring than everyone else.*

Jo decides to introduce herself and jumps down from the porch. She gets about halfway there before she realizes she's a little nervous; maybe she shouldn't talk to them. She freezes. She looks between her house and the new house and debates with herself. Does she want to say hello? How much does she really hate being bored? What if these new people think *she's* boring? What if they hate her?

Jo decides that maybe today isn't the day to talk to them. After all, her mother and father are always telling her, "Jo, you shouldn't talk to strangers." So, she's being very good by not doing it. She should just sit and read her book.

"Hi!"

Jo freezes again as she heads back to her house. She turns to see the mother coming across the street toward her. She's waving at Jo with a big smile on her face. She holds the younger girl by the shoulders. The girl looks uncomfortable.

"Um, hello," Jo says cautiously.

"My name is Tracy, and this is my daughter, Alex. We're new in town."

Jo nods. She's not sure what else she's supposed to do. Alex smiles.

"Why don't you two get to know each other?" Tracy says and gives Alex a little push. Alex stumbles forward and stares back at her mother as though she has just suggested they throw rocks through people's windows. "Go on, Alex. We'll call you back when it's dinner time."

Alex is scowling, like she wants nothing to do with Jo. Jo is offended. *What's wrong with me?* She wonders. *I'm not so bad.* But then she thinks that maybe Alex is shy;

maybe she is just as nervous, with her heartbeat pulsing in her ears, as Jo is about making new friends. Maybe she thinks Jo will not like *her*. Jo comes up with an idea to break the ice.

"Good afternoon," she says in her best British accent and an extends a hand. "I'm Joanna, but no one is allowed to call me that. So, you may refer to me only as Jo."

"Oh, Hi. I'm Alexis, but I only like to be called Alex." She shakes Jo's hand. "I guess we both have boy names, huh?"

"Yes, I guess we do" Jo giggles.

Alex and Jo stand in the street, awkwardness filling the air between them. Jo wants to look cool, but she's not sure how to do that. She's not even sure what to say.

"Do you like books?" Jo asks finally, still using her fake British accent. Her body tenses and she feels the urge to cringe, but she holds her head high. If she's going to sound like the Queen of England, she must act like it. And the Queen does not cringe at stupid conversation-openers.

"I love books," Alex admits, kicking a rock.

"Really?" Jo perks up immediately and has to remind herself that she's British. "I mean, oh? How, uh, delightful. What kinds of books?"

"Any. My Christmas and birthday presents are always

books. I have over a hundred."

"Over a hundred?" Jo asks, shocked, thinking about the measly twenty in her room. "I wish I had a hundred books. I'm reading one now. Wanna see?"

Alex looks back at her family, who are slowly unpacking a large van, and then back at Jo.

"Yeah, sure."

Jo leads Alex over to her chair on the porch and shows her the book she's reading. Alex hasn't read it yet, so Jo says they could take turns reading it out loud.

"I don't think that's a good idea," Alex says. "I'm not very good at reading out loud, and I prefer reading in my head anyway."

"Yeah, me too," says Jo. Actually, she is very good at reading out loud, but she realized almost immediately that reading for a long time with her new British accent would be difficult. She's glad Alex said no.

"When is your birthday?" Alex asks.

"August first."

"No way! Me too!" Alex's eyes brighten.

"That's so cool!" Jo exclaims.

"What do you do for fun?" Alex asks.

"I usually just sit on the porch and read."

"Oh."

This is not going well, Jo decides. She doesn't know how to salvage it, but Alex doesn't seem like she wants to go home any time soon, either. They're not talking about anything, and Jo wishes they would.

"Who's that?" Alex asks, noticing a boy walking down the street.

Jo looks up and smiles. "That's Miles Porter," she says in a whisper. "He's the cutest boy in the whole school."

Both girls watch as he walks away. He doesn't seem to notice them staring, which is good because Jo and Alex both have their mouths open in admiration.

"He's the cutest boy I've ever seen," Alex admits.

"He's in my math class," Jo tells her. "He sits at the front."

"I can't wait to start school," Alex says as she climbs back into her seat. "Especially if I get to stare at him all day."

"That can be fun, but it does get boring after a while."

"What are the classes like?"

"Well, I like school," Jo says, nervously, "and my teachers are mostly nice. My science teacher is pretty awesome. He always makes us laugh, and we get to do cool experiments. The gym teacher is scary. She always yells and makes us run laps, and I hate running."

"Ugh, me too. Running is the worst."

"But recess is fun. We have hopscotch, and sometimes we get to play with the gymnastics ribbons."

"Do you do gymnastics?"

"A little. I'm not very good, I don't think, but it's fun!"

"I like to dance," Alex says. "I did ballet when I was little, but I started taking hip-hop dance lessons just before we moved here. I hope there are classes nearby."

Jo doesn't know if there are, but she will ask her mom later. Jo's mom knows everything. You could ask her a question about a country that she's never been to, and she'll know about it. That's because she's a geography teacher. But she also teaches history sometimes. She's the smartest person Jo knows, and Jo is excited to show this to Alex.

"Who's that?" Alex asks again.

Jo watches as Miles walks back up the street, only this time it's with a girl. Jo goes to school with the girl too, and as much as she's tried, she can't hate the girl.

"That's Ariana," she explains. "She's in my math class, too."

"Is she Miles's girlfriend?"

"No, but they're very close. I think Miles 'likes-likes' her," Jo admits reluctantly. "She's the prettiest girl in school."

"Is she mean?"

Jo flops back in her chair and groans dramatically. "No," she sighs. "She's, like, the nicest person ever."

Alex looks confused as she looks after Miles and Ariana as they turn the corner and disappear.

"Why is that a bad thing?" she asks.

"Well," Jo begins, slightly nervous, "in all the books I've ever read, there's always the two girls, right? The one who is in love with the boy, and the girl who has the boy wrapped around her finger. The girl who isn't the main character is always mean. I read a book last month where the other girl sent horrible notes and made the main character feel bad. Ariana is the opposite."

Alex settles herself comfortably next to Jo now and, weirdly, it feels very normal to her. It feels as though they've never not been friends. "How is she the opposite?"

"Well, she sends nice notes. I mean, last year when I fell over and sprained my ankle, she wrote me a letter wishing me a 'speedy recovery'."

"Maybe she was pretending?"

"No. She wasn't. She really is that nice."

Alex laughs, and Jo makes a face.

"I just wish it would feel a little more like the book I read," Jo says, "but it's just not."

"It's weird that you want her to be mean."

"I know that," Jo shrugs. "But she doesn't have to be so nice about everything."

"I swear I'll never tell," Alex laughs.

They're silent for a few seconds. But before it has the chance to become awkward again, Alex takes control of the conversation and they spend the rest of the day talking about their favorite books and characters. They're both surprised when their parents call them for dinner.

"I'll see you later?" Jo asks, hopeful and nervous.

"Yeah! Tomorrow? Maybe I can come back here, and we can read or something?" Alex suggests.

"Yeah, sure! Ok, I'll see you tomorrow then!"

CHAPTER TWO

That night, Jo tells her mother and father about Alex and then helps put her twin brothers to bed. They're sleepy, so it's not as bad as it normally would be. Sometimes they can be loud and annoying, and Jo can't sleep because they're crying and screaming.

The next morning, she rushes through breakfast and then gets ready for Alex. She stares at her bookshelf for a long time, wondering if she should take the book she's reading now, or something else. Does she want Alex to think she's really smart? Should she take one of those old classic novels her father loves? Or should she take a funny book? Will Alex think she's silly for reading a book about a princess and her cat getting lost?

Eventually, unable to decide, she takes three books: one from her dad's bookshelf, a book she's read a thousand times, and the princess book that she's currently reading. She can see what Alex is reading first and then decide.

"What are you doing with all those books?" her dad asks as she is about to leave.

"I'm going to read them."

"All?"

"Maybe."

Her dad shakes his head but waves his hand, and she knows she's allowed to leave. She runs to the porch, sits down and waits.

It's a warm day. Not too hot that she's sweating, and not so cold that she needs a jacket. She loves reading outside when the weather is nice like this. It makes her feel like the girls on the cover of the classic novels, just reading and passing the time until the next big adventure comes along.

Jo has never had a big adventure like in the books, though she hopes she will one day. They sound very exciting. She'd like to rescue a princess from a tower, or fight a dragon, or hunt down bandits in forests that go on forever.

"Hey, Jo," Alex calls as she crosses the street.

Jo smiles as Alex comes up the porch steps and sits next to her.

"You looked like your head was in the clouds," Alex says. "What were you thinking about?"

"Adventures . . . and stuff." She feels silly about saying that out loud. What if Alex thinks wanting to have an adventure is childish?

"Oh cool," Alex says with a smile. "I love adventures."

Jo brightens up instantly, no longer feeling

embarrassed.

"What did you bring to read?" Jo asks, stretching her neck to see what book she's carrying.

"Oh, it's . . . well, it was a gift from my Grandma, but I really like it. It's about a princess that gets lost with her cat."

Jo excitedly pulls out her copy of the same book, and the two girls squeal with shocked surprise.

"Is that *The Notebook*?" Alex asks curiously, looking at the book on top of Jo's small pile.

"Yeah."

"I tried to read it, but it's sooooo boring," Alex says.

"It's my dad's," Jo admits. "I wanted to read it, but if we're reading this book instead, then it can wait."

The girls sit down and dive into the book. After what seems like just a few minutes, Jo's mother calls out to her.

Time can be so strange, Jo thinks. Sometimes it seems to go quickly; other times, it seems to go slowly. For example, her social studies class is supposed to be an hour, but it feels like it lasts two weeks! But on the porch swing reading a book side-by-side with her new neighbor—and friend--time goes very, very quickly.

"Jo, it's lunchtime," her mother calls from the door.

Jo snaps her book closed quickly, and she comes out of a word-induced haze. She looks around, blinking slowly as if she hadn't even realized she was still outside. "Is it one o'clock already?" she whispers, though she's not sure who she's talking to.

"Alex, darling, lunch!" Alex's mother calls from their house across the road.

"Must be," Alex whispers back. "Meet here after?"

"You bet!"

"Are you and your friend having fun?" Jo's mother asks as she cuts the crusts off the sandwiches for Jo's 2-year-old twin brothers Aiden and Jordan.

"Yeah!" Jo tells her mother all about the books they're reading and how much fun they're both having. Jo talks a lot, but when she remembers that Alex is coming back right after lunch, she shuts up and eats as quickly as possible.

"She'll wait for you if it saves you from choking," her mother jokes.

But Jo isn't willing to take that risk. She isn't unpopular; she has a few friends, but they're like, friend-friends. She's the only person she knows in the whole school who doesn't have a best friend. She's not sure if everyone else has noticed this yet, but she's reminded of it almost every day when she sees the other girls and their BFF bracelets and sometimes matching outfits. She's ready to find someone to fill that job for her. So no, she'll choke on her food if it means she gets to have a best friend.

"I'll be outside if you need me," Jo shouts through a mouthful of food. She picks up only the princess book and runs to the spot where she and Alex had been just fifteen minutes ago.

Alex wasn't there.

Jo tried not to be openly disappointed. She doesn't want to think about why Alex had decided she didn't want to hang around with Jo anymore. But she wasn't going to let it interfere with her reading time. She would have to look elsewhere for a best friend.

"Hey, did you start without me?" Alex asks happily as she runs up to Jo and sits down.

"Oh, you came!" Jo enthuses, before getting control of herself. "Cool."

"Of course I came. I was just eating, that's all."

Jo nods, as though she wasn't even the slightest bit worried.

"Where are you in the book?" Alex asks.

"Page one hundred and forty-one."

"Ooh, Ok. I'm on page one hundred and thirty-seven. Wait for me to catch up?"

Jo promises she would, and then impatiently watches as Alex reads. Watching someone read is far less exciting than reading herself. It feels like it takes as long as her social studies classes!

"Right. I'm on page one-forty-one."

Jo delves back into the book with glee.

CHAPTER THREE

The following morning, Jo and Alex meet on the school playground before classes start.

"Hey, Jo!"

Jo turns around along with the other children clustered around her.

"Do you know her?" Kimberly asks.

"Yeah," Jo says. "She's my new neighbor. You'll like her."

Jo waves Alex over, but as she's introducing her to all the people she knows, she feels oddly jealous. She doesn't want her friends to take Alex for their best friend. Alex is hers.

Jo spends the rest of the morning ignoring her other friends and talking exclusively to Alex. She's so worried that her friends will steal Alex that she doesn't realize she's acting odd. Her friends notice though. Even Alex does.

"Jo, are you OK?" Alex asks as they walk home together after school.

"What do you mean?" Jo asks.

"You're really quiet." Alex says, sounding sad. "Did your friends not like me?"

"They did!" Jo shouts. "I just…" she hesitates, not wanting to admit that she is jealous. She doesn't want Alex to think she's weird. "But what if they like you too much?"

Alex is very confused by this.

"I mean, everyone has a best friend but me," Jo says miserably, "and I don't want to be the only one without one. I wish you were my best friend."

"I want to be your best friend, too," Alex says after a pause.

Jo stops walking and gasps. "Really?"

"Yeah, really!" Both girls squeal in delight as they hug each other tightly.

Jo and Alex spend the next week doing everything together. When Alex is tidying her room, Jo is there to help. When Jo has chores to do at home, Alex comes over to help. They quickly get to know each other's families. It feels perfect, exactly like Jo had always thought having a best friend would feel like.

It was a chilly February morning, about a month after Alex moved in, that she learns that Jo did not naturally have a British accent. It had been a complete accident that she dropped the act, but Jo figured it had to happen sometime.

They had been playing hopscotch in the schoolyard

before classes started when Jo had tripped, fell, and skinned her knees. It hurt, but she didn't cry. She just stared at the bleeding scrape and then said to her group of friends—in a regular American accent--"Wow, I thought I was better than that."

Her friends had helped her up, but Alex had just watched, feeling very confused.

"You're not really British?"

Jo considered lying, saying that sometimes she tried to use an American accent, but she changed her mind at the last minute.

"No, not really. I just like the accent."

"She does it every time she meets someone new," Kimberly explains. "She's weird like that."

Jo is suddenly very worried that Alex will be offended that she lied for so long and will never want to talk to her again. But she is relieved when she sees that Alex is smiling.

"That explains why you're so good at it."

"Yeah," says Kimberly, "we kept getting new kids last year, so she spent almost three months talking like the Queen."

"You get used to it," Jenny, their tallest friend, says.

"I want to pretend to be British too," Alex declares,

with a good British accent. "Shall I call my butler to collect my tea?"

The girls fall about laughing, and then the bell rings. Alex and Jo hang back to practice their accents when Jo notices a sign on the lamp post by the school fence.

"There's a circus in town," she says. "I love the circus."

"Me too! I love trapeze artists. They're the best."

"I love the clowns," Jo says. "They're so funny."

The girls look between the school and the sign, and without saying anything to each other, they head towards the gate.

"We'll get in so much trouble," Jo says nervously.

"Only if we get caught," Alex whispers. "We'll be back before lunchtime. No one will even notice we're gone."

"Yeah. We'll be super quick."

Energized by their confidence, the two girls rush out of the schoolyard and toward the huge open lot a few blocks away. Even from a distance they can see a massive tent in the middle, all yellow and red stripes, and hear the light airy notes of a calliope. The closer they get, the louder the music is.

Once they reach the edge of the lot, Jo and Alex move

cautiously, not wanting to be caught. They sneak up to the big top's entryway and peer inside. There, inside a large circle in the center of the tent, are all the performers in the circus. They're dressed in colorful costumes and shouting to each other. Jo and Alex watch the trapeze artists far above them leaping from the podiums and swinging high through the air.

"This is amazing," Jo gasps.

"It's the coolest thing ever," Alex agrees.

"Wait until everyone at school hears about this!"

"And what are you doing?" a deep, booming voice suddenly says behind them.

The two girls scream and whirl around. Standing behind them, with hands on his hips, is the largest person either of them has ever seen in their entire lives. His arms are wider than both girls put together, and he stands at least twice as tall as either of them. He has a handlebar mustache and is wearing a leotard. His shirt proudly declares him to be the "World's Strongest Man."

Jo and Alex gulp.

"You should be practicing with everyone else," growls the strongman.

"Wait –"

"No, we're –"

Neither of them gets to finish her sentence because the Strongest Man in the World lifts them by their collars and carries them inside. Scared, and feeling distinctly like unhappy kittens being carried by their mother, the two girls are dumped in a dressing room.

"Put these on," the strongman says, throwing them two clown outfits. "Sylvia will do your make-up." Then he leaves.

Jo and Alex look at each other, neither of them sure what to do. It's not until Jo shrugs and starts putting on the outfit that it becomes a little less scary. It even becomes a little funny. By the time they have finished getting dressed, the two girls are giggling uncontrollably.

"What's so funny?" asks a new voice.

The girls go instantly silent and turn to see a woman walking into the room on her hands, her feet stuck up in the air. She's wearing a red leotard that stretches over her hands and feet and is covered in little black diamonds.

"Come on," she says, flipping and landing on her feet without a sound. "Let's get your make-up done."

Neither of the girls tries to explain that they're not meant to be there. They allow Sylvia to paint them up as clowns. The paint feels strange on their skin, and when they look in the mirror, they dissolve into giggles again. Sylvia smiles at their antics, obviously deciding that it's not worth calling them out for it.

"Alrighty, that's it. You both are done. Let's get out there and get our routines perfect."

The girls, feeling far more eager than they did before, follow Sylvia into the performance circle. They stick close to each other's side, too scared to talk to anyone; if they are discovered as imposters, they will be kicked out.

"Now then," says the Strongest Man in the World. "Let's go again, get this perfect, ready for when the ringmaster gets here. You know how I hate to disappoint him."

The members of the circus all nod in agreement and then cheer. It's obviously a tradition among them, and it sets Jo and Alex even further apart because they're the only ones who remain completely silent. No one notices, or at least no one says anything.

The Strongest Man in the World uses a remote to start the music and everyone moves off to their positions. Alex and Jo stand awkwardly where they are, not knowing what they are supposed to be doing.

"Girls, positions!" Sylvia barks at them.

They move to the side, unsure, and watch the act play out. First, the trapeze artists begin swinging from the ceiling, performing impossible stunts and putting on a beautiful show. Then Sylvia performs an impressive set of backflips around the perimeter of the circle. In the middle, the strongman lifts an anvil with "1000 pounds" written on it.

A group of clowns arrive on unicycles, honking horns, performing magic tricks and screaming silently at each other. Alex and Jo hold their stomachs because they're laughing so much. It's not until the end of the clowns' performance that Sylvia arrives behind them and pushes them into the center of the circle.

"Go on; do your bit."

Jo shrugs, seeing it as a challenge. She starts dancing, even though she's not very good. Alex joins in, doing a much better job than Jo. They can't be doing too badly, though, because the others are cheering. The music ends abruptly, and the two girls freeze when a loud booming voice fills the tent.

"Who are you?"

Striding towards them, filled with purpose and a hint of anger, is a tall, slim man with a large top hat and a red coat with gleaming, golden buttons. He's wearing knee-high black leather boots and dark black trousers.

Jo and Alex panic. Everyone else assumed that they were part of the circus, but this is the ringmaster. He knows better, and now they're in BIG trouble.

"I asked you who you were," he says, his hands on his hips.

"I'm Jo," Jo says.

"I'm Alex," Alex says.

"And what are you doing in my circus?"

"Clowning around," Jo says without thinking.

Alex elbows her sharply in the ribs and Jo has to hold back an ill-timed giggle. She isn't the best in serious situations. Never has been.

"Where are your parents?"

"At work?" Jo guesses.

"At home," Alex assumes.

Neither girl knows what time it is. There are no windows, and they're away from the doors.

"And where are you supposed to be?"

"School," the girls say together, looking at their feet.

"I have to call the police."

Alex's hand jumps to Jo's, and she squeezes far too tight. Jo kind of understands, because she's a little scared too. But Alex looks like she's going to pass out from fear. A few tears slip from the corners of her eyes and slide down her cheek.

The ringmaster notices and his face softens considerably. He kneels so that he's closer to eye level with the girls.

"Don't worry, child," he says gently. "They'll help us get you home safely. You'll likely be in trouble with your parents, but they won't hurt you. I'll go in the car with you."

Alex's grip on Jo's hand lessens, but she doesn't release it entirely.

"I'll go get your stuff," Sylvia offers.

The World's Strongest Man walks with them and the ringmaster to an office in a large trailer.

"Even though you're not clowns, that was quite the performance," the strongman says. "We need brave people. Maybe when you're older?"

The two girls smile at him nervously, and he pats their shoulders. Their knees almost buckle from the weight of his hand. He leaves and closes the door behind him.

"Sit down, sit down," the ringmaster says. "Sorry, it's a mess."

He moves some large piles of paper off two seats, and the girls sit down in them and wait.

He moves into another room and closes the door to make the phone call so the girls can't hear the conversation.

"My mom is going to ground me for years," Jo worries, putting her face into her hands and groaning.

"Do you think the police will arrest us?" Alex asks nervously, her fingers twisting in her lap.

"Of course not, we're nine," Jo replies, but she can see by Alex's expression that she isn't convinced. Alex's worry scares her. Would the police arrest two 9-year-olds, just for accidentally joining the circus? Until now she was sure the answer was no, but Alex is smart. She knows things Jo doesn't.

"The police are on their way," the ringmaster says, coming out of the room. "They've contacted your parents. You've caused quite the stir." He sits at the head of the table and looks at both girls with his eyebrows raised.

"We're sorry," Jo says quickly. "We didn't mean to. We just wanted to look. We know we shouldn't have snuck out of school, but we wanted . . . well, we wanted an adventure."

The ringmaster laughs and shakes his head. "Well, it looks like you found one! Normally, we have kids that want to run away with the circus, not just play hooky for the morning. Curiosity isn't normally the reason we have kids coming into our circus."

"Does it happen a lot?" Alex asks, looking calmer.

"All the time."

"Oh wow," Jo breathes in shock.

"Yeah. We don't accept runaways, so don't you get any ideas. You need training and to be of age to work in the circus. It's because of the law and for everybody's safety. The circus isn't just fun and games. It's hard work and hours of practice and long nights and even longer days. You have to have a big heart and a strong mind to join us."

Jo doesn't feel dissuaded from being in the circus. If anything, where there was no desire to join before, there is now. Alex, on the other hand, appears very put off the idea.

"Ah, that will be the police," the ringmaster says in response to the sound of wheels crunching on the gravel outside of the trailer. "Come on then, girls. Let's see that you get home safely."

They step outside, and it's almost dark. That's not a good sign; they both know. They're in far more trouble than they had even considered because it's late. Time speeds up in the circus. That's something they'll have to consider in the future, whenever they decide to have more adventures.

"Are you Alex and Jo?" an officer asks, as he steps out of the car.

"Yes, sir," they both say.

"Your parents are very worried."

The two girls look down at their feet, ashamed of the trouble they have caused.

"Let's get you both home then." He ushers them towards the car. "Are you coming too, sir?" he asks as the ringmaster steps towards the car.

The ringmaster leans in and whispers something in the officer's ear. The officer looks affected by what he says. He looks towards the girls, and then nods seriously. Jo wishes she knew what they had said, but then Alex tugs her hand and they both climb in.

Jo is even more scared once they are in the car and heading home. She's never done something like this before, so she has no idea how her parents are going to react. She's never been the best-behaved person, but this is the worst thing she's ever done. Failing to clean her room results in her not being given dessert. Getting a bad report card earns her a week of grounding. What if they mix the two together? No dessert and grounded? She shivers at the thought.

And then there's the shouting. Or maybe even the lack of it. Jo's mother often shouts, but her father does this silent staring thing, and it makes her stomach hurt. She hates letting them down, but it's not like she's doing it on purpose. It's just who she is.

"We're here," the policeman says.

Alex and Jo stare out of the window of the police car at Jo's house. Through the window, they can see both sets of parents sitting stiffly on the sofa. Alex's older sister is sitting on a chair with her back to the window, but it's obvious that her headphones are in.

"Ready?" Jo whispers, squeezing Alex's hand tightly.

"No," Alex replies, "but we don't have a choice."

The two girls slip out of the car, still holding hands, and they follow the officer into the house.

There's a flurry of movement at their return, and they're both dragged into a tight hug by their respective parents. There are some muffled cries, and apologies, and reprimands, but for a few precious moments, there's no shouting.

That ends the moment the hugs do. The girls stand in the middle of the room as their parents ask them what they were thinking, and why they would do something so silly. Only the police officer, the ringmaster, and Alex's sister remain quiet during this time. The twins, who were likely asleep, start to cry upstairs, and Jo's father rushes off to tend to them.

"Alexis Brianna Harper," her mother says harshly.

"Joanna Elizabeth Powers," Jo's mother says angrily.

The girls' faces burn with embarrassment and they are filled with horror: They know that once their parents have used their full names, they're in the worst kind of trouble.

That night, they're both sent to bed early. Jo knows she'll be getting her punishment when she wakes up in the morning, but for now, she's just glad to be home safe and sound.

CHAPTER FOUR

Alex has been living in her new town for three months now, and her grounding has only just come to an end. She thinks that her and Jo's parents conspired to decide how long they were grounded for because they're both free as of today.

The punishment was one of the worst Alex ever had. In addition to being grounded for so long, she was given extra chores and sent to bed early. And for the first month, she had her books taken away.

The books were the hardest part. She's always eased her boredom with reading, so not having that crutch to fall back on was a shock to her system. She cried as she watched her parents box up her books and hide them in the attic.

She'd thought that maybe she could get one at school and take it home, but her mother had called the librarian and filled her in. Alex had cried that first night without her books, right up until her sister had come into her room.

Alex was about to tell her to leave her alone, but then Chantel sat on the edge of her bed and pulled a book from her pocket. She handed it to Alex, put a finger to her lips, warning Alex to be silent, and then left. Alex cried for another reason after that.

When Alex got to school on the day she was free from

her grounding, she rushed to find Jo. She'd had to go in early to help the teachers with the design for the annual school play. She is very good at art, but she didn't think so. Mostly, Jo complained about the added responsibility. But Alex thinks she secretly enjoys it.

"We're free," she cries as she runs into Jo's arms. "We're free again!"

"Speak for yourself, I've still got to do this," Jo whines, gesturing to her paint covered clothes. "I need to get changed."

They both go into the changing room, where Jo quickly puts her school uniform on.

"Summer vacation is coming," Jo points out.

"It is. What do you want to do?"

"I dunno. Read?"

"We could," Alex shrugs, "but I want another adventure."

"Because it went so well last time?" Jo asks, though her lips curls into a mischievous smile.

"But to have a real adventure, we need vehicles."

"We can't drive," Jo says, confused.

"I'm not talking about cars," Alex laughs. "I think we should get bikes."

Jo makes a face and then sighs. "My parents won't buy me one. They wouldn't have before, but they definitely won't now."

"Then *we* buy them."

Jo is clearly still not catching on, and Alex tries to not be too frustrated. She's impatient when she has good ideas that other people can't understand. Normally, Jo is good at thinking the same as Alex, but her morning painting is obviously taking its toll.

"I think we should get a job."

Jo's face brightens the moment the words leave Alex's mouth.

"That's an excellent idea! We could . . . well, I'm not sure, but we could look up some ideas."

"I think we should try a car wash," Alex says. "Chantel did one when she was ten and she made lots of money! It can't be too hard."

"Good idea," Jo nods seriously. "I'll ask my mom tonight how we do that, and maybe she'll give us some things to use."

The two girls spend the rest of the day jittery with excitement at all the things they'll do with the bikes when they get them.

"I can't wait!" Jo squeals as they leave school. "I'll call tonight and tell you what my mom says!"

That night, Alex tells her mom their idea over dinner. Chantel doesn't say anything, which means it's actually a good idea. Normally she just grumbles something mean, which also means it's a good idea; or she outwardly laughs, which means it's a terrible idea. Alex learned to speak Chantel a long time ago. She has her own special language, though her mother says it's just "being a teenager."

"I'll help you and Jo make flyers if you want," her mother offers kindly. "We can put them up all over the neighborhood."

"Yeah!" Alex agrees enthusiastically. "I can't wait. It'll be so cool to have bikes. I want a purple one."

"You should probably check how much bikes cost before you get too excited," Chantel warns.

Alex hadn't thought to do that. After dinner, she jumps on the computer to search through her options. Jo appears online at the same time, and they both start sending each other pictures of the bikes they want.

BIKES ARE MORE EXPENSIVE THAN I THOUGHT Jo types.

THEY ARE LOTS OF MONEY BUT THERE ARE LOTS OF HOUSES, Alex reasons.

HOW MUCH DO U THINK WE SHOULD CHARGE?

I'LL ASK MY MOM

Alex jumps off the desk chair and runs to her mother, who is reading a book in the den. She reaches for her bookmark and turns to face Alex with a smile.

"What's up, Buttercup?"

"Mom, how much should we ask people to pay for a car wash?"

Her mom looks up to the ceiling, allowing herself to think. Alex patiently waits for her to formulate an answer.

"I think that you can both get away with charging $5 a car."

"Ok, thank you!"

Alex rushes back to the computer and quickly relays the information to Jo.

THAT MEANS TO BE ABLE TO AFFORD THE BIKES WE WANT WE NEED TO WASH 60 CARS

That sounds like a lot of cars to Alex, and she doesn't even know how long it takes to wash a car. Is it an hour, ten minutes, five minutes?

MY MOM SAYS THAT EACH CAR SHOULD TAKE 30 MINUTES TO WASH PROPERLY, Jo types. SO WE WOULD BE WASHING CARS FOR THIRTY HOURS.

That sounds like an awful lot too, thought Alex. They would have to spend a whole weekend washing cars. She is sure it will be worth it, but she's also certain that she'll be super tired afterward. But then, she can ride her bike for the rest of her life, and it'll be perfect, and those 30 hours won't feel like anything.

AWESOME. MOM SAYS SHE'LL MAKE THE FLYERS, Alex types. WE CAN HAND THEM OUT WHEN SHE'S DONE.

EXCELLENT. I HAVE TO GET OFF THE COMPUTER BUT SHALL WE CALL?

The two girls have gotten into a habit of calling each other every night, whether to read together or to gossip about school. Their parents were against it at the beginning of their punishment but must have started to feel bad for them being separated so much. They soon gave the girls back their phones and they haven't stopped chatting since. It's a tradition now.

COOL. TALK SOON.

Alex logs off the computer and closes it down before shouting goodnight to everyone and running upstairs. She showers as quickly as she can and then puts her pajamas on and climbs into bed. She grabs her book and her phone and settles onto the pillows. The moment she pulls the blanket over herself, the phone rings.

"Hey," Jo says once Alex has picked up. "Did you hear about Miles today?"

Alex doesn't remember falling asleep that night. But when she wakes up in the morning, her phone is on the bedside table and charging. She knows her mother did it, but it's a mystery how she manages to do it so silently, and without waking Alex up.

She stretches out and yawns before putting her feet into her white fluffy slippers and pulling on her bathrobe. She trudges downstairs, still tired, and sits at the table. Her eyes feel heavy, and she's not really ready to be awake yet. But she knows she doesn't really have a choice. She has to go to school and –

"It's Saturday," her mother shouts from the kitchen. "Why're you up so early?"

"I forgot," Alex admits sleepily. "Thought it was Friday."

She rests her head on the table and her mother lays something close to her face. Assuming that it's food, Alex reaches out, but she finds a stack of papers instead.

Alex rubs her eyes and looks at them, waking up almost instantly with excitement.

"These look great, Mom!"

Her mother then puts a plate of toast in front of her and she scoots her chair in, eager to call Jo to tell her all about the flyers. They can start planning their distribution today.

Alex is glad that she and Jo became friends. She misses her old town, her old friends, and her old school. But just like her mother promised, she did manage to make new friends. All because of Jo.

She had a best friend before she moved. His name was Greg, and they used to do everything together. They still talk sometimes, but much less now than when she first left. It makes her sad, because she doesn't know if she'll ever see him again.

Being best friends with Jo means that she doesn't think about it all that much, which is good. She doesn't enjoy feeling sad.

"What're you thinking about, darling?" her mother asks as she sits down with a cup of coffee.

"Greg."

"Would you like to call him? We can set up a playdate if you want?"

Alex nods enthusiastically and decides that she'll call Greg later on today after she's made plans to see Jo.

Today is going to be the best day ever, she thinks.

"Look what my mom made!" she shouts to Jo as they meet in the middle of the driveway after breakfast.

"They're so cool!" Jo gushes as she looks over the flyers.

The flyers are all blue and pink, with the black outline of a car in the bottom right-hand corner, and the words 'Alex and Jo's $5 car wash!' across the top of the page. In the center, there's a little box with contact details inside, and all around the edges are bubbles.

"My mom is really good at things like this. She does them for people all the time." Alex feels really proud to have a mother with such great skills. Her mother has been a work-at-home graphic designer since before she and Chantel were even born. According to her dad, she's very well respected in her area of work. Alex thinks that's very cool.

"Should we put them on doors?" Alex asks. "There's probably about a hundred houses, I think. That's much more than the number of flyers we have, but if some people don't want their car washed then maybe it's just about enough?"

"Yeah, that makes sense."

They make a hand-drawn map of the streets around them, putting X's when they know who lives there. Those are the houses that they'll definitely post to. After they've finished, they proudly present it to Jo's mom, who tells them the houses that they *shouldn't* post to. She doesn't say why, only that they shouldn't bother those people.

"Witches," Jo says knowingly as they head out into the street. "If we go to their houses, we'll be cursed."

Alex isn't sure about that, but it does make her wonder

about who really lives in those houses. They start putting the flyers in the mailboxes, crossing off the houses on their map as they go. When the girls come to the first house their mother said not to leave a flyer at, they freeze.

The front yard of the house is covered in tall weeds that reach Jo and Alex's shoulders, and the windows are dirty. The brown curtains look moth-eaten and the windows are so dark that they can't see inside.

"Alex, c'mon," Jo begs, tugging at Alex's sleeve. "It's creepy here."

Alex agrees completely, but she doesn't want to leave yet. Just because the house is creepy, doesn't mean the person living there is.

Suddenly, a woman appears in the windows, smiling at them in a sinister way.

The two girls scream and run, not stopping to look back until they're both out of breath.

"I told you so," Jo gasps. "She was a witch!"

Alex believes her now. The woman was very scary looking. She wore black clothes and lots of dark red jewelry. Her hair was black too, and wild. Alex is still shaking.

"Do you think we were cursed?" Jo asks, sounding worried.

"I don't feel cursed."

"How do we know what being cursed feels like?"

"I guess we don't know for certain," Alex admits.

"I hope I'm not," Jo says. "Summer vacation wouldn't be very fun if we were cursed."

"Sure wouldn't, would it?"

After the girls catch their breath, they continue to post flyers. The other houses they weren't allowed to go to were far less scary, but they didn't wait around to see if witches lived in them.

Once the flyers were gone, the girls ran to Alex's house, where they sat by the house phone with their map and a schedule for the following week on it. They don't have a lot of hours free during the week, but it's enough to get by.

They wait for an hour, but no one calls.

"I thought we'd be booked up by now," Jo says, disappointed.

"At least one call," Alex agrees. "Maybe people don't like clean cars?"

"Must be. The flyers were too cool for anyone to say no to."

"Why thank you, Joanna," Alex's mom says, making Jo cringe. "You girls just need to be more patient. People will call soon. Now, do you want some lunch?"

Alex nods sadly, disappointed by their failure. Sure, it's early, but that's not enough to make her feel better. She and Jo had clearly expected to have calls minutes within returning home. Alex thinks maybe the witch did curse them after all.

Alex's mother busies herself with making grilled cheese sandwiches and apple juice. Alex and Jo stare grimly at the phone, as if it was the phone's fault that they've not heard anything yet. It's certainly strange, Alex thinks, and unfair. Her sister didn't have these problems. She got calls right away. What is wrong with Alex and Jo that they didn't attract the same business?

"Here we go. Stop your worrying, Pumpkin," her mother says as she places a large plate containing both sandwiches and cups of juice on the table. She ruffles Alex's thick curly hair, something that never fails to annoy her. Her mother is the one who spends all the time trying to tame it into a style, and she has the nerve to do something like that!

"Don't pout," her mother scolds. "One day your face might get stuck like that."

Alex doubts this very much, but she doesn't bother arguing.

Once they have scarfed both sandwiches down, Alex and Jo jump up to help tidy the kitchen. They're about to collapse on the sofa when the phone rings. For a second, the two girls are frozen. But Alex's mother waves them to the phone and they both quickly run over and answer.

"Hello?" Alex says, pulling the schedule towards her, pen poised. "Alex and Jo's carwash."

"Oh, hello dear. I saw your flyer, and I would love for you to come over and wash my car today, if that is possible."

Buzzing with excitement, Alex scribbles down the woman's name, time, and address. After that, there is a flurry of calls, and within an hour, they're booked up and have more money coming in than they even needed. The girls squeal in delight, and then Alex's mom sends them to change into more suitable clothes. Jo runs home while Alex runs upstairs and puts on some grey shorts and a large black t-shirt that used to belong to her sister. When she gets back downstairs, her mother has a bucket ready with sponges and soap.

Alex thanks her mom and then takes the bucket outside to meet Jo, who is bouncing up and down excitedly.

"Come on!" Jo shouts. "Let's get this show on the road."

Alex grins and together they rush towards the first house on the list. The owner of the car is sitting on a lawn chair and offers the girls lemonade.

"Thank you, Ms. Sophia," Alex says politely.

The girls get to work quickly, but Ms. Sophia keeps talking to them. They can't seem to find a polite way to say it's making their work take longer than it needs to. What they had hoped would take only thirty minutes, actually takes forty-five and that makes them late for the next appointment.

Ms. Sophia hands the girls ten dollars, and even when they explain that it's more than they were charging, she simply shoos them away. They run to the next one and apologize endlessly to the man, who is quite grumpy at their lateness. Fortunately, he doesn't stand to chat, and they make their way through the car wash at a good pace. Unfortunately, they're still late to their next appointment, and the one after that.

By the time it starts to get dark, the girls are exhausted, and they trudge back to Alex's house. Alex takes the little plastic case with the money in it and gives it to her mother for safekeeping. The girls do not want to risk losing it.

The next morning, the girls are tired and their arms hurt. But they remind themselves that they're doing it for the bikes, and they head out to wash more cars. Sometimes the car owners are so happy with the result that they pay more than they need to. Some give them candy and lemonade, others simply mumble thanks and pay them and wave them away.

By the time it's two in the afternoon, the girls are wet and hungry. Jo's mother had offered to feed them, so they eat toast and fruit salads at Jo's house before taking on another long afternoon of washing cars. Night comes again and the girls add up all the money they've earned.

"You have almost $250 now," Alex's mom says over dinner that evening. "You're very close."

"Washing cars is hard," Alex whines. "My arms hurt and I just want to sleep all day."

Alex's mom and dad both laugh, but Alex can't find the humor in what she said. She's in pain, don't they understand?

Despite their fatigue and aches, the girls go out after school the next day and wash six more cars. They do it again on Tuesday. On Wednesday, Jo comes out of her house with a little ball of something shiny in her hand.

"What's that?" Alex asks, curious.

"I think it's called steel wool," Jo says shrugging. "But I know my mom uses it on the pans when they get really dirty, and I figured it would let us do twice the work in half as much time."

"No way!" Alex can't wait. They could wash six cars in less than two hours if this goes well. "Come on then!"

With their bucket swinging in their hands, the girls rush to their next car and get to work. Alex is tasked with rubbing soap over the car with the regular sponge and Jo will go over again with the steel wool.

Unfortunately, things go wrong immediately.

Suddenly, Jo says, "Oh no."

Alex freezes. That does not sound good at all. She looks up and finds why Jo said what she did. There's a large scratch on the side of the car, and the red paint is now on the steel wool ball.

"That's not good," Alex says nervously.

"What's going on?"

Alex and Jo turn to face Ms. Wallace, who stands in the doorway to her house, her eyes locked onto the scratch. Slowly her hands come up to cover her gaping mouth.

"Oh my," she whispers. "What happened?"

Jo looks down at her feet.

"I used this," she says, holding out the steel wool, "and it scratched off the paint."

The woman composes herself quickly, but she doesn't look happy.

"I'm going to have to call your parents," she says seriously. "They'll have to pay for the damages. Thankfully, it's not too bad."

The girls' shoulders slump in shame, and they nervously wait for their mothers to appear. Jo looks like she might cry, and Alex feels like she may cry as well. This wasn't an easy job by any means, but it wasn't supposed to fall apart like this. It's been a complete and utter failure, and they're both going to be in so much trouble because of it.

"Jo? Alex?"

Jo's father and Alex's mother both come to the house looking confused. Ms. Wallace doesn't shout as she explains what happened. Both girls are staring at the ground as the adults discuss money and things that neither of them truly understands.

"Ok, thank you for letting us know. We'll be in touch to arrange covering the costs," says Jo's father, who then walks down to the driveway with Alex's mother. Jo's father takes her hand and Alex's mother takes Alex's shoulder and they're led away from the house.

"But what about the other cars?" Jo asks, quietly.

"We'll call and apologize for the inconvenience, but I don't think that you should be doing any more car washes," Alex's mother says.

Jo sighs loudly and stares at the ground the rest of the way home. Alex's forehead is creased with worry.

We'd been doing so well, Alex thinks, *and we were so close to our goal! One little mistake and now we're left with nothing, and no way to make the money back.*

The girls are taken to their respective houses, and Alex feels much more scared now that she's alone. She follows her mother to the kitchen table and sits down without being told to.

"You're not in trouble," her mother says. "I'm not even disappointed. I should have told you to only use the things I gave you. I should have given you more instructions. This is my fault."

Alex feels fear rip through her at the thought of her mother blaming herself. It's not her mother's fault. It's her and Jo's fault. They shouldn't have tried to cut corners. They definitely shouldn't have tried to do something without their parents' permission.

"Mom, no," Alex assures. "It wasn't your fault. It was my fault. I should have told Jo not to use the steel wool. But I didn't know what it would do."

Her mother lays a hand on Alex's shoulder and squeezes tight.

"It's not the worst thing ever," her mother smiles. "It was just a scratch. You both earned enough to pay for the damages. No worries. Ms. Wallace was just a little upset at how it turned out."

Alex is still upset. But she can't do anything about that. She gives her mom a hug and goes to her room. She doesn't call Jo that night, and Jo doesn't call her. They're both upset about what happened.

However, when Alex meets Jo the next morning to walk to school together, none of the previous night's fears and worries appear to linger with her. In fact, she's almost overjoyed.

"Why are you so cheerful?" Jo asks, with her hands in her pockets.

"Because," Alex shrugs. "I dunno. Just because."

Jo gives Alex a long look, half concerned, half amused. Alex has been told that she comes off very calm most of the time, so when she catches someone off balance, it's something of an accomplishment for her. She revels in it. She doesn't want to be taken for someone who is dull or unchanging. That's not her nature. But her calmness seems to lure people into a false sense of security with her.

"Think of it like an experiment," Alex says. "We know we've got it in us to do well. We know we can make the money. We just need to find something and avoid trying to make it easier, since that's what got us into trouble in the first place."

Jo doesn't say anything in response, and when Alex twists her head to look at her, she sees that Jo is staring at the ground.

"I'm sorry about what I did," Jo says. "I didn't mean to get us into trouble. I thought I was helping."

Now it's Alex's turn to be shocked. Jo seems a little

too strong-willed and prideful to apologize for anything. And she looks apologetic too, which means she's not just saying it. She means it.

"Don't worry about it, Jo. We're in it together."

Jo beams and they hold hands the rest of the way to school, chattering about the potential money-making schemes they could cook up in the future.

When the girls get home that evening, Jo's mother is hastily putting on make-up.

"Jo, your father and I are going to the university for an awards evening, and we'll be late getting home. Dinner is in the fridge, but I need you and Alex to watch over the twins. I've already asked your parents, Alex. They said it was fine. And if you need anything, you can just call them over. They're happy to help."

Jo mutters something about never being trusted to look after the children before, and she is anxious about the prospect. Alex, on the other hand, doesn't feel nervous at all. She used to babysit Greg's baby sister before she moved. And two can't be that much harder than one, right?

Jo's parents leave, each looking like a million dollars, and Jo and Alex are left with the twins. They sit on a blanket in the middle of the living room, playing with blocks. They're quiet and are not misbehaving. But Jo's mother said that they were not to take their eyes off them, so Jo and Alex decide to take that order literally. While one of them goes to the bathroom, the other stops what they're doing to stare at the boys. While Jo is changing a diaper (something that Alex didn't even have to say she would *not* do), Alex sits with the other twin and entertains him until his brother returns. While Jo is putting the food on the table, Alex remains on the sofa, making sure the children don't get into any mischief. They have a great system going, and by the time dinner is finished, Alex is beginning to wonder just how much Jo's parents exaggerated the difficulties they would face while caring for the boys.

But all this changed the moment it was time for bed. Tricked into a sense of calm, Alex is shaken to her core by the boy's screams. They don't want to go to bed, they want to stay awake and watch TV. Jo and Alex each take a child and try to put them in their beds, but they won't sit still. They keep jumping up and trying to run away.

Jo is on the verge of tears, Alex can tell. Alex doesn't feel much better herself. *This is a complete nightmare!* She thinks. *The boys were supposed to be in bed by 7:30, but it's already 8:15. Will we be in lots of trouble for not being able to get them to bed on time? Will Jo's parents shout at us for it?*

"Please go to bed," Jo pleads with the screaming boys. "Please."

The boys pay no attention, and one escapes into the hallway and the other into the closet.

"You stay here," Jo orders Alex, flustered, "and I'll go after Aiden. I know all the hiding places."

Alex sits on the floor in front of the wardrobe and listens to Jordan's soft sniffling. She thinks he may have started crying, but she can't see his face so she can't be sure.

"Aren't you tired?" she says. "Aren't you a sleepy little bunny?"

The sniffling stops and Alex continues, hoping that she can't get somewhere with it.

"When I was small, my mama used to read me stories to help me get to sleep. How about I read you a story? Would you like that?"

She waits, and in a few seconds, the little boy with a fluff of blonde hair and red-rimmed eyes opens the door of the closet ever-so-slightly.

"Is that a 'yes'?"

He nods, and Alex smiles. *Maybe we can get at least one win out of this evening after all!*

"Once upon a time, in a land far away, there lives a young boy called Jordan and his twin brother Aiden. Together, they ruled five kingdoms. They did so fairly and justly and were kind to everyone around. They were also very handsome."

Jordan perks up at this and climbs out of the closet and

into Alex's lap. She continues with the story, adding dragons and knights and storms. After ten minutes, Jo has managed to drag Aiden in too, and she holds him on her own lap as Alex continues the story.

When Alex breaks into unsure silence, Jo saves her and together they talk and talk until both boys are sleep.

When Jo's parents return much later, they find all four of them fast asleep on the floor of the bedroom.

"Alex, time to go home," Jo's mother says, gently lifting Jordan from her lap. "Your mother is downstairs waiting for you."

Alex rubs her eyes tiredly and climbs to her feet, sleep making her unsteady. As she leaves, she sees Jo's father lifting Jo from the floor to carry her to her room.

"Hey, darling," Jo's mother says to Alex, holding out a hand. "Did you have fun?"

Alex mumbles a reply, and even she isn't sure if it was a confirmation or not. She just wants to sleep. She's not sure she's ever been this tired before in her entire life, and she's been very tired before.

"Exhausted?" Alex's mother asks as Alex comes down the stairs.

Alex hums and her mom takes her home. She ushers Alex upstairs and helps her into her pajamas and under the covers. She kisses Alex on the forehead and Alex drifts off to sleep.

The following morning on their way to school, Jo says to Alex, "My mom gave us $50 each! Look!"

The two of them jump around, laughing and grinning in excitement.

"We still have $70 from the car wash fund, so all together we have $170," Jo says. "enough for one whole bike and about ten percent of another."

"We just need to figure out how to make the other ninety percent."

"We need to think really hard. We'll find a solution."

Alex agrees. They're both smart. They'll surely find something that will afford them the long sought-after luxury of a brand-new bike for both of them. If they want it enough--and she's sure that they do-- they'll find a way. Call it stubbornness or perseverance, they'll get it eventually.

Alex and Jo spend the next few days coming up with potential money-making schemes and not finding anything of worth. Alex feels anxious about it. Summer is so close, and without the bikes, their plans will all fall through. They both need to have this summer go perfectly, because what else would they do?

Salvation came in the form of a phone call not long before summer began.

"My Gramma Gladys called," Jo tells Alex. "She said we can work on her farm, earn the rest of the money."

Alex can tell from the tone of Jo's voice that this is going to be quite the adventure.

And Alex lives for adventures.

ABOUT THE AUTHOR

L.S. Winters is a children's author and dog-lover who has loved reading all her life. Just like her characters Jo and Alex, she loves adventures, traveling and exploring new places. Her favorite vacation destination is anywhere with a beach. She lives in Northern Virginia with her three beautiful children, and she's excited to see where her new life as an author will take her.

9 781705 614853